SUMMER BREAK FOR AWKWARD BEARS

AN OBSCURE ACADEMY STORY

LAURA GREENWOOD

To keep up to date with new releases, sales, and other updates, you can join my mailing list via my website or The Paranormal Council Reader Group on Facebook.

BLURB

When Ila went on a beach holiday with her friends, the last thing she expected was to end up dating someone.

Jacob has never been a fan of parties, but when he meets a beautiful polar bear shifter at one, he finds himself reevaluating.

Can the two of them form a connection that will last beyond their holiday?

-

Summer Break For Awkward Bears is a Holiday story that's part of the Obscure Academy series. It is a light-hearted paranormal bear shifter m/f romance and is Ila and Jacob's complete story.

ONE

ILA

I CLOSE my eyes and take a deep breath, enjoying the salty scent of the sea. It's been years since I've been to the beach, which is why I jumped at the chance of coming here with some of my friends from Obscure Academy. Being away from the hecticness of the summer holidays at home for a week is just a bonus and one I'm going to make the most of.

"Earth to Ila," Georgie sings, waving a hand in front of my face.

I turn to my flatmate. "Sorry, I was lost in thought."

"Want to share it?"

I snort. "Just boring stuff about how much I love being at the beach."

"Ah, yeah, I feel you there." She looks towards where the waves lap against the sand, a wistful expression on her face.

"You're such a mermaid."

"Mmhmm, you know it," she responds. "Want to grab some ice cream?"

"Obviously, why would I come to the beach and not have it?" I ask. "And fish and chips, and fresh doughnuts, and rock candy, and..."

Georgie chuckles. "I thought you were supposed to want to try to bulk up for the winter, not the summer."

"Well one, that's bear-bears, not shifter-bears, and two, what part of *polar* bear did you miss? It's always winter for me."

"I don't think that's how it works," Georgie responds, linking her arm through mine.

"It is on holiday. When else can I do anything I want to?" I let out a satisfied sigh just at the idea of that.

"Now you're speaking my language."

We turn the corner and enter the ice cream shop that's blasting cold air out into the British August heat. We're lucky that the weather has mostly behaved for our planned holiday, to the point where it's almost too hot.

"Hey, Georgie!" A second mermaid I recognise from some of Georgie's MerSoc parties waves as we enter.

"Hey, Fiona," she responds. "I see you had the same idea as us?"

Fiona nods, her shimmering green hair falling in front of her face. "Ice cream is always a good idea," she points out.

"Mmm, true," Georgie responds, already eyeing up the various flavours as if she doesn't already know what she wants.

"Are you guys coming to the party later?" Fiona asks, looking between the two of us.

"What party?" I haven't heard anything about one, but then again, I don't know as many people as Georgie does. The mermaid is much more of a social butterfly than I am. Or a social fish, though I don't think that's the right way to say it.

"Oh, we're having a party tonight at the house we've rented," Fiona says. "I thought the invite had gotten out to most of our friends. It's nothing fancy, just bring your own bottle."

"Sounds good," Georgie says. "Right, Ila?"

I nod. "It'll be fun."

"I think so," Fiona responds. "My flatmates know how to throw a party."

Georgie chuckles. "Yeah, they do. Have you ever been to one of theirs?" she asks me.

"I'm not sure," I respond. "Maybe? It's hard to keep track."

Fiona lets out a light laugh. "It's hard for me too, and I live in my flat."

The queue moves forward and she heads to the front.

"We don't have to go if you don't want," Georgie says when no one else is listening.

"We're going," I say firmly. "A party sounds good, and isn't that why we're here? We're supposed to be having a good time and letting off steam before term starts again."

She lets out an amused snort. "You mean before we go back to another year of partying amongst the occasional study session."

"Something like that," I say with an amused smile. "Besides, I know you don't want to stay away. You'll probably want to spend the evening searching for what's-his-name."

"I don't know what you're talking about," she mutters.

"Mmhmm, of course you don't."

"It's just a summer fling," Georgie says.

"That's not a promise that you're not going to try finding him later," I respond.

"All right, I thought it might be fun if I could find him and then we could go down to the water and have some fun."

I raise an eyebrow. "I have lots of questions and I don't think I want to know the answers."

"Nothing like that," she assures me. "Oh, look, they have banana cream." She points to the display.

I wrinkle my nose. "Are you really going to order that?"

"We don't have flavours like that in Merton," she says. "Just kelp, and sea salt caramel, that kind of thing."

"Even so, you could pick a better flavour. Chocolate chip, or strawberry..."

"How is strawberry any better than banana cream?"

"Ah-ha, so you admit that banana cream is bad?" A triumphant feeling fills me at her admission. Surely no one buys banana cream?

"I do nothing of the sort, just order your ice cream," she says, gesturing to the waiting cashier.

"Hi, I'd like a honey macadamia in a waffle cone, and a banana cream in..." I pause and look at Georgie.

"In a sprinkle cone," she finishes, a childlike glint of glee on her face.

I roll my eyes.

"Coming right up, that'll be four pounds twenty," the cashier says.

"Thanks." I pull out my card and touch it to the machine. "You can get the next ones," I say to Georgie.

"Or I'll get the drinks later."

"Sure." It doesn't really matter to me, I know that it'll even out eventually.

The cashier hands over the cones to us.

"Thanks," Georgie says.

I turn around and bump into the guy behind me.

He reaches out to steady me, his hand reassuring despite the fact I have no idea who he is.

"I'm sorry," I say, looking up and meeting a pair of deep chocolate-coloured eyes. I take a deep breath, surprised to find the familiar scent of bear shifter on him.

"No problem," he mumbles, glancing away almost as if he doesn't want to say that.

"Enjoy your ice cream," I say, stepping back.

"I don't have ice cream."

I blink a few times, trying to work out a way to respond to that. "Well, enjoy your future ice cream, then." I give him a tight smile and follow Georgie out of the ice cream shop.

"What was all that about?" she asks.

I look back and shrug. "No idea." I eat some of my ice cream. "But it's fine, it's not a big deal."

"Not when there's ice cream to be had and outfits to plan for the party tonight," Georgie responds.

"That we do." We carry on down towards the promenade, where some of our other flatmates are in the arcade. That'll be a fun way to pass the afternoon before we head to the party. And is it really a beach trip without at least some time and money wasted in the arcades?

TWO

ILA

MUSIC BLARES from the sound system, leaking out into the street. It's a good job that it's mostly holiday rentals in this part of town, otherwise, we'd probably be driving people crazy with the parties.

Georgie opens the front door and steps inside. "Hey, Byron," she says, waving to our other flatmate.

"Hey," the sprite responds in his usual cheery manner. "Good to see you here."

"You mean because you're a traitor shacking up with your girlfriend for the summer instead of hanging with us?" Georgie throws back.

I chuckle. "Leave him be, we all knew he was going to pick Essie over us."

"Hmm, true." A satisfied smile quirks at the corners of Georgie's lips. And no wonder, after all the dancing around each other Byron and Essie did at the beginning of the year, they've been inseparable for months.

"Cups are in the kitchen, there's plenty of mixers too," Byron says, gesturing vaguely towards a door at the back.

"Not quite bring your own, then," I joke.

He chuckles. "One of Essie's flatmates is a stickler for organisation, she'd never let us get away without providing something, and it's easier to agree and chuck in a tenner than it is to argue."

"You're not wrong there," I respond, shooting a knowing glance at Georgie. There's no denying that she's that person in our flat.

"Hey, guys," Essie says as she steps next to Byron and places a hand on his back in a casual show of affection.

Byron's face lights up at the arrival of the dark-haired fae, which isn't a surprise considering how mopey he was when she ended things before Christmas. I'm glad they're back together, even if it's for our benefit. He was almost unbearable in his misery.

"I'm going to go get myself a drink," I say, not fancying the idea of sticking around while they act all couply. I'm used to it, but it's still not exactly my thing.

Georgie nods, her attention on someone over the faes' shoulders. I look over in that direction, only mildly surprised to discover that her summer fling is leaning against the doorframe. At some point, she's going to have to tell me more about him.

"Have fun," I sing-song to my friend.

"I...oh you know what, I'm going to."

"Maybe you can take that swim you talked about earlier," I tease.

She sticks her tongue out at me and walks over to where he's waiting even as she does. So predictable, and it only confirms that I'm right to go and get myself something to drink rather than hang around and be a fifth wheel.

I chuckle and head towards the kitchen. If she's going to be busy, then I'll just go and find one of my other friends.

I pull out my phone, noticing a message in our flat group chat from Holly. I tap the screen so it opens.

< About to start Beer Pong, anyone want in? We could use another member on our team. >

< I am! > I type back quickly and hit send. <

Just getting a drink and I'll be there. Which room are you in? >

< The conservatory. We're starting in five minutes, > Holly responds.

< I'll be there. > I slide my phone back into my pocket and step into the kitchen, happy that I have a destination. I smile to some of the cheerleaders I recognise from when they drink at our place and head towards a table groaning with all kinds of mixers. Byron wasn't exaggerating when he said they were prepared.

I grab one of the cups and fill it with a generous splash of the raspberry vodka I brought with me.

"Can you pass the lemonade?" someone mumbles from beside me.

Without thinking, I reach for the open bottle and turn to hand it to them, freezing in my tracks as I do.

"You!" I can't keep the surprise out of my voice.

Surprise flits over the guy's face. "Ice cream girl."

"I have a name."

"I don't know it," he points out.

Right. That would help before I get too annoyed at him for not knowing who I am. "Ila."

"Jacob."

"Here's your lemonade, Jacob," I say, holding out the bottle.

"Thanks." He takes it from me and pours some into his cup.

"Don't you want to mix it with anything?" I ask.

"No."

"If you've run out, you can have some of mine." I lift the bottle of vodka.

Confusion flits over his face. "No."

"Okay." I smile and turn back to making my own drink, topping it up with lemonade once he's set it down.

He stands there, but doesn't say anything.

"Are you all right?" I ask, a little at a loss for what else to do.

"You didn't insist."

"Insist on what?"

"That I drink," he responds, sounding as confused as he looked.

I fit the cap back onto the lemonade and turn to face him. "I figured you either didn't want to, or you felt like you'd had enough. It's not my place to force you to drink. That would make me cruel."

"Most people would." There's still a hint of confusion in his voice, but if I'm not mistaken, there's also a hint of relief.

"Then most people are idiots," I respond.

He chuckles. "Are we supposed to say that?"

"If anyone's trying to force you to drink, then yes, they're idiots."

"No one is forcing me."

"Okay, then that's good. I don't need to be all growly at them then," I joke, assuming that he's been able to sense that I'm a bear shifter just like I can sense his inner bear.

Jacob frowns, not seeming to understand.

"Well, enjoy the rest of the party," I say lamely.

"Yes."

I give him a weird half-wave, slightly confused about what's happening, and why I suddenly feel so weird about the situation.

I head out of the kitchen, looking back over my shoulder without realising what I'm doing. Jacob is still standing at the table with his cup of plain lemonade. I'm not sure what to make of him, or the whole interaction, but there's a part of me that wants to talk to him more and work out precisely what it is that's going through his mind.

I shake my head to rid myself of those thoughts. He's just a guy who happens to be at a party with the rest of us. That probably means he goes to Obscure Academy, but other than that and being bear shifters, we probably don't have anything in common, and it's better if I just let our interaction fade from my memory and focus on what I'm really doing here. Having fun with my friends.

THREE

JACOB

I SHOULD NEVER HAVE AGREED to come to the beach. I'm not sure what possessed me to say yes when Ceb asked me to come, but next time, I need to say no, even if I don't want to miss out on time with the friends I've made at the academy, which is the main reason I ended up agreeing.

I check my phone to make sure I'm at the right place and look up at the wooden arch, pleased to find that the business name across the top matches the address on my phone.

I step inside and head to the front desk.

"Welcome to The Shift Space," the receptionist

says brightly. "What can I do for you today? We have spaces for small, medium, and large shifters, and a freshwater pool that will fit most aquatic creatures."

"Bear," I blurt.

She smiles and nods, but I can tell it's fake. "One ticket for the medium room, then. You pay on the door, and it's the fourth one to the left. You'll find lockers inside for your belongings, and changing rooms if you need them."

"I don't."

"Okay then." She looks a bit uncomfortable. "Just down the hall." She waves in that direction, clearly anxious to get rid of me.

I don't take it personally. A lot of people act that way, and I know better than to ask them about it.

I head down the hall, counting the doors as I go and coming to a stop at the one with *medium* written on the door. A touch screen sits next to it, asking me to click the button and pay. I pull up the payment app on my phone and wait for it to beep. The door clicks and swings open, letting me step inside.

Just as the woman said, lockers line one side of the room, and the other has changing cubicles like the ones I'd expect to see at a swimming pool. I ignore them, like most shifters, my clothing is of the spelled variety and will shift with me when I change forms. My phone and wallet are another matter, meaning that the lockers are still a necessity.

I'm relieved when I find the third locker on the second row still available and empty my pockets into it. I pat myself down to make sure that I'm not carrying anything I've forgotten about. The last thing I want is to lose an important possession because I shifted with it in my pocket.

Satisfied that I'm not about to do that, I close the locker and put in a code. A light breeze comes from the door that leads to the shifting space, hinting that there's at least one outdoor component. That's nice, I always prefer it when it's like that. I don't mind the indoor shifting spaces too much, but they're never quite as satisfying as the ones that have greenery.

And trees. I love climbing them when I'm in my bear form, even if many of the varieties we have in the UK aren't suited to bear paws.

I head outside and take a deep breath, letting my shift take over me. Dark fur bursts from my skin, and my whole body gets bigger. I sniff at the ground, able to sense all kinds of smells that I couldn't before.

A loud splash sounds from the far left, and I turn my head, surprised to find a polar bear frolicking in a stream. Nothing should surprise me when it comes to shifters, I know that all animals have a shifter counterpart, and that there are several mythological creatures that can be shifters too. My best friend is a hellhound and I don't find that strange, so why should this shifter be any different?

And yet despite knowing that, the sight of a polar bear playing in a stream during the summer is a strange one. Normally, they like to stay out of the sun.

They must sense me watching as they lift their head and look in my direction. I can't tell from so far away, but I think there's some curiosity in their gaze.

I'm probably imagining it. No one here is going to be paying me any real attention. Which is normal. Sometimes, friends come to shifting spaces together and will interact with one another then, but strangers will ignore one another. Which is one of the reasons I like shifting this way instead of trying to sneak off into the woods or anything like that. If I could do this completely in private, then I would, but I wouldn't even know where to start finding somewhere to do that.

I scan the rest of the space to try and work out where I want to go. A copse of trees draws my attention and I start making my way over to them with the intent of climbing one of them. It'll be good to stretch out my paws and challenge myself to some terrain that I'm not used to.

Within minutes, I can feel the stress of the last couple of days seeping away. I know that most people would consider a holiday like this to be relaxing, but for me, it just doesn't work like that. At least now I have a chance to let off some steam properly.

I hook my paws over one of the branches and start the process of climbing up it. I'm sure I look ridiculous to anyone watching, it doesn't feel like a particularly elegant way of getting up a tree.

I find a large branch that I think will support my weight and lie down, hanging my paws off each side. The light breeze ruffles through my fur while the sun warms it. There's something truly wonderful about the feeling, like it's nature's way of ensuring that shifters feel at one with the world around them, even if the rough bark of the tree scratches against my skin.

A chime sounds, signalling the changing of an hour. I ignore it. There isn't a time limit on how long I can stay here, so long as it doesn't creep beyond their closing time, which means I'm only beholden to my own boredom and to what I want to do later in the evening.

Which if I ask my friends is a party, whereas I

like the idea of just relaxing and avoiding as many people as possible.

After what feels like another half an hour, a rumble of hunger has me climbing down from the tree and heading back to the entrance. I shift back to human as soon as I'm within sight of the door and step inside the locker room to come face to face with a girl I recognise.

"Ila," I say in surprise.

"Hey, Jacob. I thought that was you." She brushes some blonde hair behind her ear and gives me a friendly smile. "I was just going to head to the pier and get myself some fish and chips. Want to join me?"

Surprise flits through me. "You want to go for food with me?"

She shrugs. "Sure. Though if fish and chips isn't your thing, we can do ice cream. Or fresh doughnuts. I love the smell of them, don't you?"

"Yes."

"Then we can get some of those, if you want." She cocks her head to the side as she waits for an answer, but it doesn't feel demanding. I like that.

"Okay."

It's her time to be surprised, or at least I think she is given the expression on her face. "Cool, I just need to grab my phone." She gestures to the lockers.

"Same."

"I guessed, you've just come in from outside." Her friendly smile makes me think that her words aren't meant to mean anything more than they do.

"Right."

"Your fur is a lovely shade of brown, by the way," she says. "I wish mine was like that. I always feel so conspicuous when I'm around other shifters. Like everyone can see every patch of dirt on me because of the white."

My eyes widen as the realisation hits me. "You were the polar bear."

She nods. "I thought you realised? I could tell you were a bear shifter from the moment we met."

"Oh." That explains some things.

She turns to the locker and gets out her bag and a thin cardigan. "Are you going to get your stuff?"

"Right, yes." I grab it, a little confused about what is happening, but liking the idea of spending some time with her. She seems nice, though I know that people can be deceiving.

"Have you decided what you want?" she asks. "Fish, ice cream, doughnuts, all of them?"

"Is all of it a good idea?"

Ila shrugs. "I'm always hungry after a shift. Aren't you?"

I nod. "That's why I came down from my tree."

"Then all of it sounds good. We can share if you don't want a full portion. Though we don't have to. I know people can be particular about that."

"I'd rather have my own portion."

"Great, then that's what we'll do." The way she smiles at me makes me think that she genuinely means what she's saying. Which is nice. Not everyone is like that. "Shall we?" She heads towards the door, only pausing when she realises that I'm not following.

I smile and head to the door with her. I need to eat, and there's something about the pretty polar bear shifter that makes me want to spend time with her, even if I can't explain why.

FOUR

Ila

THE SALTY SCENT of the sea reaches my nose and I take a deep breath. "I love this smell," I say as we make our way down the path that goes alongside the waterfront. It's not very late, which means that there are a lot of people around, but they don't seem to be paying very much attention to us, which is just the way I like it.

Jacob gives me a strange look. "What smell?"

"Of the sea. Do you like it?"

He shrugs. "I suppose it's okay."

"Glowing praise. So what do you like, other than climbing up trees?" I ask.

"What makes you think I like that?"

"Because an hour ago, you entered the shifting space, climbed up a tree, and then seemed to take a nap. I don't know anyone who would do something like that without liking climbing."

"Ah. Yes, I like to climb trees."

"Do you have a favourite?"

"Tree?"

"Mmhmm."

"Elm," he responds, sounding a little sheepish.

I nod to myself as I consider his answer. "That's a good choice, I like the way they branch out from the trunk."

"You don't have to humour me," he says.

"Why would I be humouring you? I think elm trees look magnificent." Genuine confusion flits through me.

Jacob glances away, clearly conflicted.

"Okay, we can talk about something else."

He looks back at me, confusion written all over his face. "You would change the conversation just like that?"

I shrug. "I asked you for food because I thought it'd be nice to talk to you, I don't want to make you uncomfortable."

"Oh. So you really do want to know about my favourite kind of tree?"

"If that's what you want to talk about. My favourite is the willow tree, I like the way the leaves look like they're falling. It reminds me of rain."

"I like elms because of the way the branches grow outwards," he responds. "And because the bark was used to fight a famine in Norway in the early eighteen hundreds."

"Huh, I didn't know that." We arrive at the fish and chip shop I came to the other day. "Do you like this one?"

I'm almost surprised when he nods. "This one is good."

"Or would you like ice cream first?"

He chuckles. "I almost think that you want ice cream first."

"Maybe I do," I respond.

"Then that's what we should do."

"There's the shop we met in? Did you like the ice cream from there?" I ask.

"It was okay."

"More glowing praise," I quip. "Let's try somewhere else."

"There's one there." He points to a big plastic ice cream cone standing outside a hole-in-the-wall style shop.

"Perfect. I can get a Mr Whippy."

"Did you know that they're supposed to be the

perfect combination of fat and sugar to make it extra tasty?" he asks.

"Nope, but that explains why they're irresistible," I respond, joining the back of the queue. "Do you want a flake with yours?"

He shakes his head. "I'd like a fudge stick."

"Oh, I've never tried that. Maybe I should too, especially if you think that's what's tasty."

"What if you don't like it?" he asks.

I shrug. "Then I won't finish it."

The line moves forward and I order us both some ice creams. I hold the first one out to Jacob who takes it gingerly.

"Is it okay if I pay?" I ask, though I'm not sure why. I think I can sense that he's not entirely comfortable in a social situation, and I don't want to make him more so by taking a choice away from him that I don't have to.

"Erm, if you're sure?"

I nod and pull out my phone, holding it above the machine until it beeps. "You can get the doughnuts in a bit, if you want," I suggest.

He nods, reassuring me that I made the right decision in asking him about it. I'm not sure precisely what Jacob's deal is, but I don't really mind either. It doesn't take much for me to be nice about the situation.

"Thank you," he says.

"You're welcome." We start walking again. "Want to go down to the beach?"

He nods. "But I'm keeping my shoes on."

"I'm guessing you don't like the feel of the sand between your toes?"

"No."

"Does it work? Keeping your shoes on?"

Jacob chuckles. "Not really, no."

"Will you hold my ice cream while I take mine off?"

He takes it from me and waits quietly while I kick off my shoes and put them in my bag. I'll probably regret it later when I have to clean the sand out of it, but otherwise, they'll end up getting in the way.

"Thanks," I say as he hands me back my ice cream.

We head onto the beach and I let out a soft sigh as the sand squidges down under my feet. I don't get to the beach often enough. I lick my ice cream, only realising after I do that this might not be the best thing to eat in front of someone I barely know. But it's too late for that now, so I keep at it, enjoying the fluffy and smooth texture that comes from the Mr Whippy machines.

Seagulls caw overhead and the sea crashes

against the sand a few feet away from us. The early evening sun provides a nice backdrop to a stroll on the beach. It almost makes it romantic.

"I didn't expect you to be a polar bear," Jacob says.

I raise an eyebrow. "And what did you expect me to be?"

"Erm..."

I chuckle. "So I'm guessing you didn't think that question through."

"I'm not very good with small talk," he murmurs.

"I can work with that. And I don't mind what you say."

"I think I expected you to be a pixie or some other kind of fae," he admits.

"I don't have pointy ears," I say, tucking my long hair behind my ear, partly because my attention has been brought there, and partly to prove that it's true.

"Not all fae do though, right?"

"Honestly, I've never spent much time staring at fae ears to know," I say.

"Right, because that would be rude," he says.

I raise an eyebrow. "So you have?"

"Not on purpose," he admits. "It's just that it's better than looking in their eyes."

"I don't think fae magic works by looking at people." I eat more of my ice cream.

"Oh, it's not them, I just don't like making eye contact with people."

I file the information away so that I can use it to try and make him more comfortable. "What kinds of fae don't have pointy ears?" I ask, mostly to keep the conversation going.

"Ottermaaner don't."

"What are ottermaaner?"

"Oh, erm, they're a kind of fae who can turn into otters."

"Wouldn't that just make them shifters?" My curiosity is piqued even if this isn't the kind of conversation I thought we'd be having.

"I think a lot of them say they are to avoid confusion," Jacob responds. "But I believe they're the same class as kitsunes and phoenixes."

"Ah, I see." I pull the fudge stick out of my ice cream and bite into it. "Mmm, this is good. I might have a fudge stick next time I get an ice cream too."

His face lights up. "I'm glad you like it."

I take another bite and smile, hoping he realises that I'm being sincere. "I never got to ask who you're on holiday with."

"Maybe I live here."

"You don't seem to like the seaside anywhere

near enough for that," I point out. "Besides, you were at a party for Obscure Academy students last night. Unless you're in the middle of a summer fling with someone, then you're probably a student yourself."

"Ah. I'm here with my flatmates. No summer fling."

My stomach does a little flip at the response, though I can't explain why. "Same. Well, not your flatmates, I'm here with mine. I never thought I'd be coming on holiday with them so soon after we met, but it's nice."

"It is," he agrees. "Even if there is sand everywhere."

"Tell me about it. There was sand in the bathtub when we arrived at our rental house."

"They probably didn't clean very well."

"Certainly not as well as they should have done," I agree. "We did our own deep clean before we used anything." Mostly because Kerry made us, not because it matters too much to the rest of us.

"That seems smart."

I finish eating the cone of my ice cream and dust my hands against the skirt of my sundress. "I could have the fish and chips next. Sandwich them with the doughnuts. What do you think?"

"I could eat more," he says.

"Great, then let's head back up the ramp and we'll find some proper food." I gesture to the sand-covered exit from the beach up ahead.

"Do fish and chips count as real food?"

"Fish is a protein. And mushy peas are a vegetable." Even as I say it, I feel like the logic is weak, but it's fun to at least pretend that it's good for us.

He wrinkles his nose.

"Not a fan of mushy peas?" I ask.

"The texture is all wrong."

"Which is the best bit!"

"I can't agree with you." There's a small hint of amusement in his voice that I don't think has been there before. Maybe he's starting to warm up to me.

"Then it's a good job you don't have to. What do you prefer with yours? Curry sauce? Gravy? The gravy is never as good as the stuff my mum makes, but I know some people like it."

"Just plain with a bit of salt," Jacob says.

"Also a good choice."

He frowns and studies me intently.

"What?" I ask.

"You're not what I expected," Jacob says.

"What did you expect?"

"I don't know. Not this."

"Well, if *this* is a good thing, then thanks, I

guess." I smile and head in the direction of the nearest fish and chip shop. I've no idea what's going through Jacob's head, but despite it all, I'm finding myself enjoying his company, and that's all that really matters.

FIVE

ILA

I HUM to myself as I climb the steps back to the house, undeniably warm and fuzzy all over. I had no idea that I was going to run into Jacob in the shifting space, but it's been a fun evening nonetheless. I didn't quite pluck up the courage to ask him if he wants to do it again, but maybe I will next time I run into him, which will no doubt be soon with all of the parties going on. I suppose that's an advantage of there being so many students here all at the same time.

I punch in the keycode and step inside, hearing a

cheer from the kitchen. I head in that direction and find myself smiling as I walk in on Dean, Kerry, and Holly playing what seems to be an energetic game of snap.

"Mind if I join?" I ask, already slipping into the seat beside her.

"Be our guest," Holly says. "The more the merrier."

"She's in a good mood because Chris finally managed to get the day off work tomorrow," Kerry tells me.

"That's great, is he coming tonight?" I ask the elf.

Holly shakes her head. "I hoped he could, but he doesn't get off work for another couple of hours."

"That's late. I thought he worked at the bathstore?"

"He does, but they're doing this weird thing where the shopping centre is staying open after hours, which means that his supervisor has asked him to stay. He agreed but said that if he stayed tonight, then he needed a couple of days off, so at least there's that," Holly explains.

"I'm sorry he couldn't come sooner."

"Me too, but I've been having fun without him. I don't need my boyfriend around all the time cramping my style."

I chuckle. "You mean losing beer pong is style?"

She groans. "Don't remind me or the hangover is going to come back."

"Can't Grace make you a hangover cure?" Kerry asks. "Pixies are good at that, right?"

"I hadn't thought to ask her," Holly responds. "I'll ask her when she gets back. You're not the only one sneaking out on dates."

"I wasn't on a date."

"Really? Because Dean saw you on the beach with a guy earlier," Kerry says, bemusement in her voice.

Surprise flits through me. I didn't realise any of my friends had been around while I'd been spending time with Jacob. "It wasn't a date, I ran into someone I met at the party last night and we got talking and went for food."

"*Ran into.*" Kerry puts air quotes around the words.

I roll my eyes. "No, it was a genuine run-in. We were at the shifting space and we happened to be in the changing rooms at the same time."

"It's starting to sound more and more like a date," Dean points out. "I've had a run-in or two of my own in the changing rooms if you get my drift." He waggles his eyebrows.

"Which ones?" Kerry asks. "That way I can

avoid using them. Or send cute guys your way, whichever you prefer."

"I don't need any help with the cute guys, thanks," Dean responds. "I can find them all on my own."

"It's not that kind of changing room. There are just some lockers and space to put things if you don't want to shift in your clothes, and a couple of cubicles if you want to shift in private," I explain, knowing that none of them are shifters. They've probably never had to think about what it's like for us before we head out into a shifting space.

"You're making the story very dull," Kerry says. "Hopefully, Georgie will have some more interesting stories to tell us when she gets back."

"I didn't realise she was out," I say.

"That's because you haven't been keeping track of the group chat." Holly reaches out and taps her phone.

"Oh, I think my phone died." I pull it out of my pocket and try to turn it on.

"Here." Dean grabs the cord coming from the plug socket and holds it out to me.

"Thanks." I stick it into my phone, feeling the familiar sense of relief when the battery icon pops up to show that it's charging. "So what are the headlines?"

Holly starts dealing the cards to us all.

Kerry shrugs. "Nothing new. I think Georgie's been as subtle as a rom-com heroine when it comes to her crush on that selkie."

"I didn't realise that's what he was," I say.

"A yummy selkie," Dean says. "I'd take his sealskin off if you get what I mean."

"Ew, never say that again," I respond. "Ever. You're officially banned from saying a single word to him too."

"Don't worry, Georgie made that very clear already. I pointed out that if it was just a fling, then surely she wouldn't care, but she wasn't a fan of that logic." He shrugs, clearly not caring about that.

"I wonder why," I mutter.

Dean shrugs and picks up his cards. "I'm not about to steal her man. That goes against all kinds of rules."

"I'm surprised you have any at all," Kerry quips.

"Hey, no fair. I have plenty of rules," Dean responds. "I wouldn't date you."

Kerry sticks her tongue out at him and he blows her a kiss.

I smile to myself, amused by their antics, just like I normally am when they get going.

"I guess we'll find out more about him at the

party tomorrow," Holly says. "Georgie said they're going together."

"What party?" I ask.

"Oh, didn't you hear? A few of the sports teams had some social budget left over and decided to rent out the party room in one of the hotels near the pier. Everyone's going." Holly picks up her cards, but doesn't start the game.

"Who is everyone?" I ask.

"She means everyone who goes to Obscure Academy and happens to be in town," Dean answers for her. "It's going to be awesome."

"How are there even so many students in the same place in the first place?" Holly asks.

"I guess everyone started talking about how cheap it is here, and then they want to go to the same place as their other friends, and suddenly there are dozens of us in one place instead of dotted up and down the country," Dean responds. "Or maybe it just feels like that because we know a lot of people."

I lean back in my chair, contemplating what he's saying. He isn't wrong. We do seem to know a lot of people, even if I've never considered that to be true. And I know for a fact that we chose this place to rent our beach house because it's where several of our other friends were coming.

I suppose lots of other friend groups had the same idea. But in the end, I don't think that's a bad thing. We're all here because we want to have fun, and if all of our friends from across the academy are here too, that's just going to make that easier, not harder.

Besides, there's a small part of me that's hoping that Jacob will be at the party tomorrow and I'll get to spend more time with him. I don't know for sure that he will be, but considering he was at the party a few days ago, I have to assume that he's going to be.

Then again, perhaps it's best not to wait for this kind of thing. I pick up my phone and swipe to open it. I head to the ObscureConnect app, hoping that it's not going to take too much effort to find Jacob.

Thankfully, someone seems to have had the foresight to make a group for everyone here at the beach, and I soon find the dark-haired bear shifter.

I click on his profile and send him a friend request. I should have asked for his number before we parted ways earlier, but I didn't think about it. Once he responds to it, I'll send a message to ask if he has plans tomorrow, with my day completely free until the party, I might as well make use of it.

And there's a big part of me that feels excited at the prospect of getting to spend more time with

Jacob. He was good company, and I'm looking forward to learning more about him.

I just hope that the feeling is mutual.

SIX

Jacob

I CHECK my phone for the tenth time since I arrived at the arcade, half expecting to find a message from Ila saying that she's cancelling on me. I'm not sure why I took her up on the offer of going to the arcade today, but as soon as I read her message, I had my answer.

"Hey!"

I turn around and smile at the sight of the blonde shifter walking towards me. She's wearing another sundress that makes her look exactly like she's on her summer holiday. Which I suppose she is.

"Hi," I blurt out after realising that I need to say something and can't just stand staring at her. That's rude, even I know that.

"I'm glad you got my message." The expression on her face suggests that she's telling the truth.

"You did send it directly to me," I point out.

"Then I'm glad I didn't send it to someone who looks exactly like you and has your name," she says.

"Has that happened to you before?"

"No, but it did happen to a friend. It's enough to worry me about it. I should have asked for your number yesterday, but I didn't."

"You can have it now," I say.

"I'd like that." She pulls out her phone. "Do you have a code I can scan?"

I nod and pull it up, holding out my phone to her so she can do it.

"All right, all done," she says brightly.

My screen lights up with a message from an unknown number containing a single bear emoji. I smile. "Is that meant to be me or you?"

She shrugs. "You, I suppose. There isn't a polar bear emoji."

"Yes, there is." I click on the message and pull up the emoji board, finding the right one and sending it back to her.

"Huh, so there is. You learn something new every day."

"I'm glad I could help."

"I'm going to update all of my screen names to have this at the end now," she says brightly, slipping her phone back into her bag.

I frown, unsure whether she's being serious or not. I suppose it doesn't matter much.

"So, what's your favourite game?" she asks, gesturing to the arcade.

"Erm, I don't know. My mum didn't like them so we never came," I admit.

She blinks a few times. "You've never been to a seaside arcade before?"

I shake my head.

"Okay, then we've *got* to start with the two pence games." She reaches out to grab my hand.

The moment she touches me, I freeze.

Horror flits over her face and she pulls her hand back. "I'm so sorry, I should have asked."

"It's okay," I murmur.

"No, it isn't. I'm sorry, I didn't realise." She smiles at me in a way that I think is meant to be reassuring. "Do you have a pound coin?"

"I think so." I dig my hand into my pocket and hold it out to her.

"Great." She takes it and heads to a bright

yellow machine. She grabs one of the plastic tubs from the top and sticks it under the spout. The moment Ila puts the pound coin into the slot, the crashing of other coins comes, and several two-pence pieces start shooting from it.

Well, I suppose there are going to be fifty of them.

"Here you go." She holds the tub out to me. "Just let me get mine, and then we'll pick a couple of machines." She repeats the process with a pound of her own, filling an identical tub.

She leads me over to where a line of glass cabinets with blinking lights and annoying sounds stands. All of them have trays of two pences and some prizes sitting on top of them, none of them looking like they're particularly good quality.

"Which do you like the look of?" she asks. "This row seems to be dinosaur themed, that one has clowns, and the other one seems to be emoji themed."

"We should do that one," I say, smiling slightly at the thought of the polar bear emoji she didn't know existed.

"Okay."

We head over to the row that seems to match the description she gave me. Sure enough, lots of the prizes seem to be themed around emojis.

"I don't think I understand the point of the prizes," I admit.

"No one does," she says with a slight laugh. "They're meant to keep you playing. Look, this one has a good chance of us winning. Oh, and the one next to it doesn't seem too bad either." She moves down one and picks up one of the coins from her stash.

"What do I do?" I ask.

"Get your coin and wait until the right moment to release it. I think it's when the drawer at the back is all the way in, that way your coin pushes on the others when it lands and doesn't just end up on top of them."

I nod and wait until the right moment before releasing the coin. Sure enough, when the drawer moves forward and back again, it pushes on the other coins in the machine, but doesn't knock any over the edge.

Next to me, Ila loads up her next coin and lets it go. Her machine lets out a loud trilling noise.

"Oh, this one seems to have tickets," she says, pointing to a stream of them that have just shot out of the machine. "I guess we can save them up and pick a good prize at the end."

"That sounds good." I let my next coin go, and follow it quickly with another one.

This time, a whole row of coins gets pushed off the edge and they clatter down into the prize tray.

"So we just keep going?" I ask.

She nods. "Until you run out of coins and don't want to get any more, or until you win the prize you want."

"Great, I want the pen," I say, pointing to an emoji-covered pen that isn't far from the edge of the tray.

"Good choice."

The way she smiles at me makes me think that she's really having fun and enjoying hanging out with me, which isn't something that I realised would happen when we met. Not because of Ila herself, but just because of how these things normally go.

"Ah, I'm out of coins," she laments after another few minutes. "I'm going to go get some more. Want me to get you some too?"

I shake my head. "I think I'm all set."

"Okay, I'll be right back." She waves and heads off in the direction of one of the yellow machines. A small part of me worries that she isn't going to return, but I dismiss it.

Some people may be like that, but I don't think Ila is one of them. And she's the one that suggested we met up today in the first place, which means she's unlikely to let this go without spending the full day with me.

I let a few more coins fall into the machine and get a trickle of others back in return. Perhaps I should have taken her up on the offer to get me some more.

I drop another one, this time pushing another lot over the edge. The pen moves forwards and teeters over the edge, almost falling off, but not quite.

Ila returns and rattles her tub of coins. "I'm ready to try and win the stress ball I don't actually want and will never use," she jokes, pointing to the winky face emoji stress keychain that's sitting close to the edge of hers.

"Do you need a keyring though?"

"Not really. But I'll probably still use it. Sometimes, it's nice to be reminded of fun days out. I see your pen is close to the edge." She points to the front of my machine.

I nod. "It's probably going to write horribly."

"More than likely. But you'll also probably smile every time you see it and end up keeping it in your pen pot for years."

"Yeah, I think so." I can feel the corners of my lips pull up into one now, even though I haven't even won it yet. I don't think that matters. I could win nothing today, and it's still going to have been a worthwhile day spent.

"Oh, I meant to ask, are you going to the party later?" She tucks a strand of blonde hair behind her ear.

"What party?"

"Okay, so that's a no."

"I might not have been paying attention when my friends told me about it," I admit. "So it's not a definite no."

"I can message you the details later, if you want. It's just a party for the Obscure Academy students in town."

"That sounds fun." I don't know why I say that, I don't think it sounds fun at all. Except perhaps for one thing.

She raises an eyebrow. "You didn't seem particularly enamoured with the last party we were both at."

I grimace. "It'll be fun if you're there?"

"Excellent answer," she responds. "I'll message you later."

I nod, realising that for what's probably the first time ever, I'm actually looking forward to a party.

Sometimes, strange things happen, and this is definitely one of them.

SEVEN

ILA

THE PARTY IS in full swing by the time we arrive, and I quickly lose my friends amongst the assembled students. There seem to be several drinking games already going on, but I don't pay them any attention. I'm more interested in finding the person I actually want to spend time with.

Not that I don't want to hang out with my friends, it's just that I get to do that all the time, especially as we're all staying in the same house. But after the fun-filled afternoon I spent with Jacob, I'm more interested in finding him and seeing if it was a one-off, or if it could be something more.

I never saw myself as a summer fling kind of person, even if I have nothing against the idea of them. But perhaps that's going to change.

I make my way from the main party room into one of the side rooms. I'm not sure how the organisers have managed to afford this, even with the leftover sports societies' social budgets, but I'm not complaining too much, it looks like a great party.

My gaze lands on a sofa with a familiar figure sitting on it and nursing a drink. I find myself smiling and heading over in Jacob's direction. "Is this seat taken?" I ask, gesturing to the other seat.

He looks up, relief written plainly on his face. "It's all yours."

I sit next to him, being careful not to encroach on his personal space. He didn't seem particularly happy when I tried to grab his hand earlier, though from the way he spoke to me and his body language, I have to assume it's because he doesn't particularly like being touched, which is something I should have checked before I tried to. At least it doesn't seem to be personal.

"You don't like parties very much, do you?" I ask.

He sighs. "No."

"Why did you come if you don't like it?"

"You asked me if I was."

"Oh." I reach up and tuck a strand of hair behind my ear. "I didn't mean to make you do something you didn't like."

"I know. But I wanted to."

"Would you like to get out of here?" I suggest. I don't like the idea of him being uncomfortable when he's the person I want to spend time with.

"Haven't you only just arrived?"

I nod. "But I don't really need to be here."

"You'll miss the party if we leave," he points out.

"That's true. But I can go to a party any time I want. It'll be a fun night, but at the end of the day, it's just a party."

Uncertainty crosses his face, as if he isn't sure whether to say yes or not. I'm going about this all wrong.

"Do you know what the first thing I thought about when I found out about tonight was?" I ask.

"No."

"I wondered if you were going to be here," I tell him. "I had a lot of fun hanging out with you yesterday, and again today. So I wanted to spend more time with you tonight."

"Why are you telling me this?"

"Because I like you? You're fun to be around." Nerves flutter in my stomach as I say the words. I'd normally dance around the issue for longer, but Jacob feels as if he's a straight-to-the-point person.

"No one has ever called me fun before."

"Then they clearly haven't been paying attention. I had a lot of fun with you. So much that I went back to the house I'm staying at and did this." I open my bag and pull out my keys, revealing the squishy emoji stress ball keyring I won earlier.

A wide smile spreads over Jacob's face. "You used it?"

"Yeah, I did. Have you not used your pen?"

"I wrote a postcard to my Grandma with it. We were right, it wrote terribly."

"You didn't have to use it."

"Yes, but today was fun."

"It was. And if the party isn't the place for us to have more of that, then I'm okay with leaving and going somewhere else. We never got those doughnuts yesterday, maybe we could go and find some," I suggest.

"You really like doughnuts, don't you?"

"Only at the seaside when they're fresh," I respond. "Elsewhere, they'd have to be really good for me to choose them over other things."

"What would you normally get at a bakery?"

"I'm not going to answer that until you agree that we're going to leave the party and go for a walk down the promenade," I say, getting to my feet and holding out my hand before I realise what I'm doing.

I'm about to pull it back when he reaches out and takes it, giving me a hesitant smile as he does.

My heart skips a beat and feels as if it swells several sizes. I don't know him well enough for me to feel like this is a big deal, and yet I know that it is, and I appreciate it all the same.

He gets to his feet and lets go of my hand, but the gesture has already changed things, I can sense it in the way he's moving. "I'd like a walk," he agrees. "And a slushie to go with the doughnuts."

"Interesting choice. Which colour do you like best?"

"Shouldn't you be asking about flavour?" he asks.

I shrug. "They all taste the same."

"That's not true. Blue is definitely sweeter than red," he responds.

"I can't even tell if you're joking or if you really think that. We should get both of them so that we can try."

He chuckles. "You'll find that I'm right."

"And if you are, I will concede defeat gracefully and will never question slushie flavours ever again."

"That is a satisfactory outcome."

"Let me just message my friends so they know I'm leaving," I say, typing out a quick message in our group chat as I do and hitting send.

"Good idea." He gets his phone out, I presume to do the same.

"All right, shall we?" I gesture towards the door, excited at the prospect of getting to spend more time with Jacob.

"Are you sure you don't want to stay at the party?"

"I'm sure." I smile at him. "There'll be a lot more parties for me to go to in the future, I don't mind missing this one."

Something like relief crosses his face, though I'm not sure if it's because we're not staying here, or because I want to spend time with him.

Or maybe he just really wants doughnuts. I'm not sure it matters when the result is the same.

EIGHT

JACOB

THE PROMENADE IS NOWHERE near as busy as it was yesterday, though there are still plenty of people about, several of whom seem to have been drinking from the way they're stumbling around and shouting.

"Here's one," Ila says, pointing to a food stand with the lights still on. "Mmm, I can smell the doughnuts."

The sweet smell of frying dough is impossible to ignore. My nose may not be that much better than a human's when I'm in this form, but I don't think anyone would be able to miss it.

"They have a five-for-two-pounds deal, is that okay?" she asks.

"It's a shame they don't have a deal with the slushies too."

"I can try haggling," she says. "They do it on that business reality show, do you know the one?"

"With the centaur billionaire?"

"Yes, that's the one. I started watching it with my dad when I was eleven. They haggle all the time."

I chuckle. "Badly."

"Ah, so you do watch."

"Yes. I enjoy hearing all of the ridiculous things they say about what they are to business," I respond.

"Did you see the latest one? There was that leprechaun who said he was the King Midas of product creation." I can hear the excitement in her voice as she realises that I'm interested too.

"I liked him," I admit. "Not at first, I thought he was really arrogant, but he grew on me."

"He did on me too, but I didn't like him as much as the winner."

"Who was that again?" I ask.

"It was a witch who wanted to open a business selling sweets that change colour and flavour according to what you're in the mood for."

"That sounds like a good packet of sweets," I say.

"Doesn't it just? I like the idea of it. I keep meaning to order some," she admits. "I'm more of a chocolate person than a sweet one, but I'm curious, know what I mean?"

I nod.

"What can I get for you?" the man behind the counter asks as we reach the front, breaking through our conversation and causing a surge of disappointment within me.

"Hi," Ila says brightly. "Can we have five doughnuts and two slushies? But can we have four straws, please?"

The vendor gives her a funny look, but turns to get things ready for her. Ila pulls out her phone and goes to her payment app.

"These are on me," I remind her. "You said when you bought the ice creams that I could get the doughnuts." And I don't want her to think that I break my promises. It's important to me that Ila knows that she can trust me.

"So I did. I forgot about that already, you could have gotten away with it."

"I don't want to." I get my own phone out and wait for the man to hand Ila our order before letting the app take care of payment.

"I saw a bench overlooking the beach," she says. "Should we go there?"

"Sounds good."

She smiles, making my insides squeeze together in the process. There's something about Ila that makes it easy to spend time with her, and I want more of that.

"Okay, so red or blue first?" she asks, holding the drinks out to me.

"Hmm, I'll have blue."

She holds it out to me and I take it from me, our fingers brushing as I take it. For a moment, I expect myself to tense up, but it doesn't come. Just like it didn't when I took her hand at the party.

Ila's eyes widen, though I'm not sure precisely what causes it. "Here are your straws," she mumbles, handing two of them to me.

"Why did you ask for four?"

"Because I didn't think we were at the sharing straws stage," she quips.

"When would we be at that stage?" I ask.

"Erm..." She clears her throat. "Well, I guess we'd be there if we were dating." Her cheeks flame red, though I'm not sure precisely *why*.

"Is this not a date?"

She frowns. "I don't know, is it?"

"I suppose it depends on what we're counting as a date," I say.

"I guess you have to know it's a date in order for it to be one," she replies. "If two people like each other and want to spend more time together then it could count. But only if they agreed."

"Then this could be a date," say.

She bites her bottom lip. "I think I'd like it if it was."

"And you did ask me to meet you earlier to hang out," I point out. "Technically, that would count as a date too."

"I don't think that counts, that was just us hanging out. Or are you trying to say that you want us to be on our second date?"

"Or our third, if you count the first time that we got food."

She lets out a good-natured laugh. "Now you're really stretching it. I think we can agree that *this* is a date, and that the other two were just two people hanging out together and having a good time. They were pre-dates."

I'm surprised by the way her words make me feel, like I wanted her to admit that that is what this is. I hadn't really thought about it myself until just now.

"And the next time we meet up?" I ask.

"Let's see how today goes," she responds.

I nod, satisfied that the answer makes sense and is what I want it to be.

"But we're still not at the sharing straws stage, so you're sticking to your own." She tears the paper coating off one of her straws and sticks it into the red slushie. "Out of interest, what's your stance on mixed slushies?"

"They're wrong," I say adamantly. "The colours shouldn't touch anything."

"Even if purple is a much more natural colour for a drink?" She takes a sip of her slushie and blinks a few times. "Oof, brain freeze."

"You're a polar bear," I point out.

"So? You think I don't get cold?"

"I honestly don't know. Do you?" I ask.

"Of course. That's like asking a mermaid if she ever gets wet."

I frown. "What?"

She wrinkles her nose. "I don't know, it sounded good in my head."

"It didn't when you said it out loud."

"Nope, it really didn't. Okay, switch slushies?" She holds out the red one to me and I swap her for the blue one I'm holding.

She sticks her other straw into the blue one and takes a sip. "They're exactly the same."

"They're not," I respond.

"Okay, then which is your favourite?"

I frown. "Blue."

"Then let's swap back."

"Are you sure?" I ask.

"If you have a preference and I think they taste the same, then it's a no-brainer. You should have the one you like better. Now give me the red one."

I've never thought about it that way before, but I do as she asks and hand her the red one back.

She undoes the bag with the doughnuts in it and holds it out to me.

"Did you get any napkins?" I ask as I take one, sugar spilling everywhere.

"I did." She digs into her bag and pulls out a crumpled mess of them. She peels one off and hands it to me before getting a doughnut for herself.

She bites into it and lets out a small squeak of appreciation. I eat my own quickly, enjoying the fact that it's still warm from the fryer even if it makes the sugar sticky.

I look back at Ila and try to smother a laugh.

"What is it?" she asks.

"You have sugar on your cheek."

"Oh." She lifts one of the napkins and tries to wipe it away. "Did I get it?"

I shake my head.

She tries again.

"Still no. Will you let me help?" I hold my hand out for one of the napkins, unsure where the offer came from, or why I think it's a good idea.

"Go for it." She places one of them in my hand.

I reach out and use the napkin to wipe the sugar away, trying not to think about how hard my heart is racing, or how contrary to the way I normally act this is.

I pull back and smile at her. "All done."

"Thanks." She touches her cheek, seeming a little lost in the moment. I guess that means that she was as affected by it as I am, which is reassuring. I'm not imagining how I'm feeling. That's always a good thing.

I clear my throat and take another drink, mostly for something to distract myself.

"I love this time in the evening," Ila says. "It's always so beautiful when the sun is setting and the colours are so varied across the sky." She lets out a loud sigh.

"It is pretty," I agree. "It's like a painting."

"It is," she says. "A romantic one."

"That's true." I glance down. "Can I hold your hand?" I ask.

She looks at me, surprise written on her face. "You want to?"

I nod. "I think so."

"Okay." She lifts her hand and holds it out to me.

For a moment, I question whether this is the right thing for me to do, but then I look out at the sea and how beautiful the entire picture is, and I know my answer. I reach out and entwine my fingers in hers, enjoying the way it feels a lot more than I expected.

Ila smiles at me, her whole face lighting up, and I realise that the view isn't the most beautiful thing around. And I feel lucky that she seems as interested in spending time with me as I am with her.

NINE

ILA

THE LIGHT IS QUICKLY FADING, but I don't want my time with Jacob to come to an end, which is hard when I know we have to go home at some point.

"Did you know that this beach has a shifter-friendly zone?" he says.

"It does?" I can't keep the excitement out of my voice when I ask, and for good reason. It's rare that places have that, and even more so when they border on the sea. "Where is it?"

"Erm, I don't know." He pulls out his phone and taps a few buttons before moving it so that I can see. "Not far, a couple of minutes walk at most."

"How do you feel about going there?" I ask, knowing that it's a risky thing for me to ask. But he's already seen my shifted form, it's not like he's about to be surprised to discover that I'm a polar bear.

"I could shift," he says. "Though I don't think there are many trees on the beach."

"No, but there's the sea." I let out a wistful sigh. "Do you know how long it's been since I last shifted in the sea?"

"No."

Right, obviously he doesn't. We only met one another a few days ago, though it already feels like longer.

I jump to my feet. "We should go."

He joins me and glances at my hand.

I lift it and hold it out to him, not knowing whether or not I should. But he asked me to hold it before, so perhaps he'll be willing to try it again.

The moment he slides his hand into mine, I feel a sense of giddiness overtake me. I'm not imagining anything, the way he's acting definitely suggests that he can sense whatever this is between us just as well as I can.

He checks his phone a few times as we make our way down the beach, but it's an easy walk, made even better by the slight breeze coming from the sea, and the way the water is playing at the edge of the sand. I can't wait for my paws to be the ones digging into it instead of my feet. There's really nothing like it.

"We're here," he says, gesturing to the huge blue and white *Shifter Zone* sign in front of us. There's a whole list of rules underneath it, but nothing that I'd consider even slightly unreasonable.

"We should find a good rock to stash our stuff behind," I say.

"Or we could just use one of those lockers." He points to where a row of them sits by the wall that separates the beach from the promenade.

"Or we could do that," I agree. "Someone clearly thought this through when they designed it."

"It makes a change. I went to a shifting space once that turned out to be nothing more than a field," he says.

I wrinkle my nose. "That's no fun."

"It isn't," he agrees.

We head to the lockers and I open the first one I come to. "Want to share?"

He gives me a strange look.

"What is it?"

"I don't mind sharing, but can we use this one?" He points to another of the lockers.

I shrug. "Sure."

I open it up and put my shoes and bag inside while Jacob studies me with a confused expression on his face.

"What is it?" I ask.

"You didn't ask why?"

"I don't need a reason," I point out. "If that's the locker you want to use, then that's the one we'll use, it really doesn't make much of a difference to me. Should I be questioning it?"

"I like using the third locker on the second row," he admits.

"That's as good a reason as any."

"Even if I can't explain it?" he asks.

"I don't need an explanation," I assure him with a smile, shutting the locker once he's put his things inside. "Oh look, it's one of those fingerprint ones. We should both do it so we can access it."

I press my thumb down on the scanner and then click the button that'll allow him to do the same. We make our way further onto the beach and I take a deep breath. The breeze plays with the end of my hair and the hem of my dress, but it's a pleasant experience and will be even more so when I turn into my bear form.

I step further away from Jacob to give us both the space we need. I didn't get a good sense of how big his bear form was the other day, but I can't imagine it'll be much smaller than mine.

The shift comes easy to me, and my form changes in an instant. My clothes change form with me, and not for the first time, I find myself glad for enchanted clothing. I hope the witch who invented the spell that makes clothes change forms with shifters is living a very happy retirement right now.

My paws hit the sand and I stretch them out. It's not quite the same as walking on snow, but it's a good close second. I glance over my shoulder to find Jacob's brown bear form standing and watching me. He's actually smaller than I expected, though I'm not sure if that's because I'm bigger than most bears, or if it's because I misjudged things. I don't suppose it matters.

I let out a small roar and nudged my head in the direction of the sea. I don't want to waste this opportunity to play in the sea. It's rare that I get a chance to do this and I want to make the most of it.

Jacob bobs his head up and down in a gesture that I assume is an affirmation, though I don't know him well enough to be sure. That will probably come once we've spent more time together, both in our shifted forms and in our human ones. I'm looking forward to finding out more about him.

I set off towards the sea, my paws throwing sand up into the air as they hit the beach. I'm sure I don't appear as the most graceful creature in existence, but I don't care. There's something freeing about being in this form. It's a part of me that I don't always get to express during the time I spend as a human. No one expects the sweet little blonde to be able to transform into something as big as my polar bear form.

The waves rush against my paws and I can feel the excitement over being here rush over me. I glance over my shoulder in time to see Jacob reaching the water. He seems a little hesitant at first and I wonder whether I made the right decision in leading him here, but then he charges into the water, spraying it all around in the process. Some of it hits me and I shake my whole body to try and get it off.

He lets out a low growl that I think is meant to be playful.

I raise myself onto my hind legs and then let myself fall forward. Water shoots away from where I land.

Jacob eyes me warily and then copies, a blur of dark brown fur as he plays with the water.

Amusement and unbridled joy fill me. This is childish beyond belief, but it's fun, and that's what being on holiday is all about. Right now, I don't have to worry about academy work, family stuff, or any of my other commitments, this is just about having the time of my life and nothing else.

I'm glad I've found someone that I can enjoy that with.

TEN

ILA

DESPITE NOT HAVING KNOWN Jacob for very long, I'm excited at the prospect of meeting him for another walk down the beach. I like his company and it's clear that the feeling seems to be mutual.

I wave the moment I see him heading towards the spot we've agreed to meet at, my heart skipping a beat. I smooth down the skirt of my summer dress, hoping that he doesn't think I'm boring because they're the only thing I've been wearing this week. But they're the perfect choice for a week in the sun and I won't have anyone tell me otherwise.

"Hey," he says as he approaches.

"Hi," I respond. "So, what seaside activity are we going to do today?" I ask.

"Hmm, I'm not sure we have many left," he responds. "We've played in the sea, gone to the arcades, and eaten plenty of seaside food."

"The doughnuts were the best." And not just because we ate them while the two of us had what felt like a moment.

"They were good," he agrees.

"So, what does that leave us? I think there's an aquarium if you want to head there, or we can build a sand castle. Maybe take a walk?" My suggestions come out thick and fast, as if I'm not sure what I want. Which is probably accurate, I'm not entirely sure. All I know is that I want to spend more time with him and that I'm not ready to go home tomorrow.

"If we walk, then we can talk more," he says.

"Then that's what we'll do," I respond with a smile.

To my surprise, he holds out his hand to me.

"Are you sure?"

He nods. "I liked it when you held my hand before."

"I believe that technically, you were the one to initiate that," I point out. Though I don't mind. He's clearly not the most comfortable when it comes to physical affection, so doing things on his terms is important. Especially if I want things to last.

We start walking as soon as I lace my fingers through his and entwine them with one another. I like the way it feels to hold his hand and feel the warmth against my own.

The afternoon sunshine has brought a lot of people outside, and the beach is heaving with people, just like it has been on the other days. I'm not sure exactly who it was that decided we were coming on holiday on this particular week, but they made the right decision. It wouldn't have been half as fun if it had been raining the whole time.

"How long are you staying here for?" I ask Jacob.

"Another couple of days. You're leaving tomorrow, right?"

I nod. "Really early too. The problem with a student budget."

"Ah, the cheapest train home?"

"Yep. It was twenty quid instead of seventy, I wasn't about to pass up on that saving, though I'm starting to regret it now."

"Why?" he asks.

"Because it means that I have to spend less time with you." I try not to feel too embarrassed by the admission. I wouldn't normally be saying this so early, but with my impending train, I feel like I need to get it out in the open.

"Ah."

"I know it's lame to admit it, but this has been the best part of my holiday. I've really enjoyed it." I glance away, not wanting to hear if he doesn't feel the same, though I suspect that's not going to be the case.

"It's been the best part of mine too," he agrees. "I didn't expect to enjoy it here as much as I have."

"Then I'm glad I could help."

"There is one thing that could make it better," he says slowly, as if he isn't sure how I'm going to respond to whatever it is that he's going to say.

"Oh?"

He gives my hand a gentle tug and I turn around to face him, coming to a stop.

"What is it?" I ask as I meet his gaze, the seriousness in his eyes a little worrying.

"I think I'd like it if I could kiss you."

My heart flutters in response, almost feeling as if it's going to burst out of my chest in the process. I manage to nod. "I think I'd like that too."

The way his whole face lights up chases away any thoughts I have that he doesn't feel the same way as I do about the time we've spent together, and it makes me eager to find out what's to come next for us.

Jacob steps closer and lifts his free hand to touch my cheek. I search his eyes, hoping to make sure that he's still comfortable with this. I don't want him to do anything he doesn't want to. Though from the expression on his face, I don't think this counts as that.

My eyes flutter closed as he leans in and brushes his lips against mine. The touch is so gentle that for a moment I worry that I'm imagining it, but then he lets go of my hand and uses his to pull me closer.

I let myself disappear into the kiss, enjoying how purposeful it is. This isn't a kiss shared with a near-stranger in a dark club, or at the end of a first date. This is a kiss that I know means something.

We break apart and I can see from his smile that he's thinking the same kinds of things as I am.

"So, when term starts in September, how do you feel about a date there?" I ask.

"I'd like that."

"It feels very far away."

Jacob chuckles. "It's two and a half weeks, that's barely anything."

"Mmm, I suppose not. And I can message you, right?" I ask.

"I'd like it if you did."

"Then that's what I'll do." I pause. "Can I kiss you again?"

"I'd like that very much."

I wrap my arms around his neck and press my lips against his, enjoying the closeness that comes with it. No matter what happens next, I'm certain that we've found something special, and I'm not going to let it go.

EPILOGUE

Ila

Three Weeks Later

There's a skip in my step as I make my way to the fountain, knowing that Jacob is going to be there waiting for me. It's taken some getting used to the fact that I can see him so often again, especially after we had to spend a couple of weeks only communicating via messages and one single video call. But now we're back at the academy, we're able to make the most of one another's company.

I turn the corner and my heart skips a beat at the sight of his familiar figure waiting in front of the fountain. I raise my hand and wave, hurrying over to where he's waiting.

"Hey," I say, going up on my toes to press a kiss against his cheek, which feels like a huge deal considering the first time I tried to touch him he flinched back.

"Hi. How was class?"

I shrug. "It wasn't particularly interesting," I admit. "You know what it's like at the start of term, everyone's more interested in doing their outlines and telling you about what they expect from you in terms of coursework."

"I like that they do that," Jacob says. "That way I know what I have to do."

"I like knowing it too, but they could email us instead of wasting class time on going through that stuff. We pay enough to come here, the least they can do is actually use all of the teaching time to do just that."

He chuckles. "Do you always spend your time thinking about how much teaching time you're owed?"

"No, just a little bit of it," I admit. "But you know I'm right."

"I do. But this is also the way things are." He rests a hand on the small of my back, sending a small thrill through me at the show of affection. I know we're taking things slowly, which seems especially important when it comes to making sure he's comfortable, but it still makes me feel good.

"I know, and there's some comfort in that. You're not the only one who likes knowing what to expect."

"So, what are we going to do tonight?" he asks.

"Well, there's this party I've heard about..."

He groans. "Okay."

"I'm teasing," I promise. "I know you don't like going to parties, I'm not about to make you go to one of them. I actually thought we could just hang out and watch a movie or something."

"That does sound better than a party," he agrees.

"All right, then let's go pick up some snacks, then we can go back to mine and pick a movie?" I suggest.

"That sounds perfect to me."

He leans in, and I close my eyes, knowing that he's about to kiss me and welcome it. I can't believe that this has all come about because of a summer holiday, but it's the best souvenir I can think of.

Thank you for reading *Summer Break For Awkward Bears*, I hope you enjoyed it! If you haven't started the Obscure Academy series yet, you can with *Shifting Forms For Clumsy Felines:* http://books2read.com/shiftingformsforclumsyfelines

AUTHOR NOTE

Thank you for reading *Summer Break For Awkward Bears*, I hope you enjoyed it!

Several of the side characters mentioned in the story have stories of their own, including Holly in *Secret Santa For Grumpy Elves*, Essie and Byron in *Trading Names For Polite Sprites*, Ceb in *Team Building For Friendly Hellhounds*, Grace in *Minor Inconveniences For Annoyed Pixies*, and Fiona in *Flipping Tails For Seasick Mermaids*.

I'm also planning for Georgie to have a book of her own, that may involve a selkie and a second chance romance!

If you want to keep up to date with new releases and other news, you can join my Facebook Reader Group or mailing list.

Stay safe & happy reading!

- Laura

You can find out more about each of my series on my website.

Obscure Academy

A paranormal romance series set at a university-age academy for mixed supernaturals. Each book follows a different couple.

The Apprentice Of Anubis

An urban fantasy series set in an alternative world where the Ancient Egyptian Empire never fell. It follows a new apprentice to the temple of Anubis as she learns about her new role.

Cauldron Coffee Shop

An urban fantasy series following a witch who discovers a cursed warlock living in a teapot.

The Shifter Season

A paranormal Regency romance series following shifters as they attempt to find their match. Each book follows a different couple.

Forgotten Gods

A paranormal adventure romance series inspired by Egyptian mythology. Each book follows a different Ancient Egyptian goddess.

Amethyst's Wand Shop Mysteries (with Arizona Tape)

An urban fantasy murder mystery series following a witch who teams up with a detective to solve murders. Each book includes a different murder.

Grimm Academy

A fantasy fairy tale academy series. Each book follows a different fairy tale heroine.

Purple Oasis (with Arizona Tape)

A paranormal romance series based at a sanctuary set up after the apocalypse. Each book follows a different couple.

Supernatural Snow Fair

A paranormal romance series based at a Christmas/winter fair. Each book follows a different couple.

Speed Dating With The Denizens Of The Underworld (shared world)

A paranormal romance shared world based on

mythology from around the world. Each book follows a different couple.

Broomstick Bakery

A complete paranormal romance series following a family of witches who run a magical bakery. Each book follows a different couple.

Grimalkin Academy

A complete urban fantasy academy series following a witch cursed to create kittens every time she does magic.

The Paranormal Council

A complete paranormal romance series following paranormals trying to find their fated mates. Each book follows a different couple.

You can find a complete list of all my books on my website:

https://www.authorlauragreenwood.co.uk/p/book-list.html

Signed Paperback & Merchandise:

You can find signed paperbacks, hardcovers, and merchandise based on my series (including stickers, magnets, face masks, and more!) via my website: https://www.authorlauragreenwood.co.uk/p/shop.html

ABOUT LAURA GREENWOOD

Laura is a USA Today Bestselling Author of paranormal, fantasy, urban fantasy, and contemporary romance. When she's not writing, she drinks a lot of tea, tries to resist French macarons, and works towards a diploma in Egyptology. She lives in the UK, where most of her books are set. Laura specialises in quick reads, whether you're looking for a swoonworthy romance for the bath, or an action-packed adventure for your latest journey, you'll find the perfect match amongst her books!

Follow Laura Greenwood

- Website: www.authorlauragreenwood. co.uk
- Mailing List: https://www. authorlauragreenwood.co.uk/p/book-sign-up.html
- Facebook Group: http://facebook.com/ groups/theparanormalcouncil

- Facebook Page: http://facebook.com/authorlauragreenwood
- Bookbub: www.bookbub.com/authors/laura-greenwood

Milton Keynes UK
Ingram Content Group UK Ltd.
UKHW010853280923
429557UK00004B/154